Dory meets a clownfish named Marlin.
He is looking for his son, Nemo. Nemo is lost, too!

Mr. Ray is Nemo's teacher. Dory likes to help him lead the class, but she's not very good at teaching.

Mr. Ray wants to show his students the stingray migration.
But as they watch, Dory almost gets pulled away in the undertow!

The stingrays help Dory remember something important, but she quickly forgets.

Suddenly, Dory finally remembers her parents!
She asks Marlin and Nemo to help her find them.

Marlin and Dory go to visit their sea turtle friends, Crush and Squirt. They can help Dory find her parents!

Dory remembers the name of her home: the Jewel of Morro Bay, California. Crush gives them a ride on his shell along the California current.

When they arrive at the Jewel of Morro Bay,
Marlin asks some hermit crabs for help.

Suddenly, Dory remembers something—she asked the same hermit crabs for help when she was young!

Just then, a giant squid appears and tries to capture Nemo!

When Dory tries to help Nemo, she gets caught in some trash.

Suddenly, a large human hand plunges into the water and grabs Dory!

The Jewel of Morro Bay is really the Marine Life Institute—the MLI. Dory is given a tag, which means she will be moved to Cleveland!

Inside the MLI, Dory meets an octopus named Hank. Hank has only seven tentacles, which makes him a septopus!

Hank wants to go to Cleveland, so he agrees to help Dory find her parents in exchange for her tag.

Dory studies a map of the MLI and tries to remember where her parents live.

Suddenly, Dory remembers collecting shells with her parents when she was a little fish.

A staff member walks by holding a bucket.
Dory is sure it can help her find her parents—it's destiny!
She leaps into the bucket and gets carried away. . . .

The bucket is for Destiny, a whale shark—and she remembers Dory! They used to speak whale to each other through the pipes in the MLI.

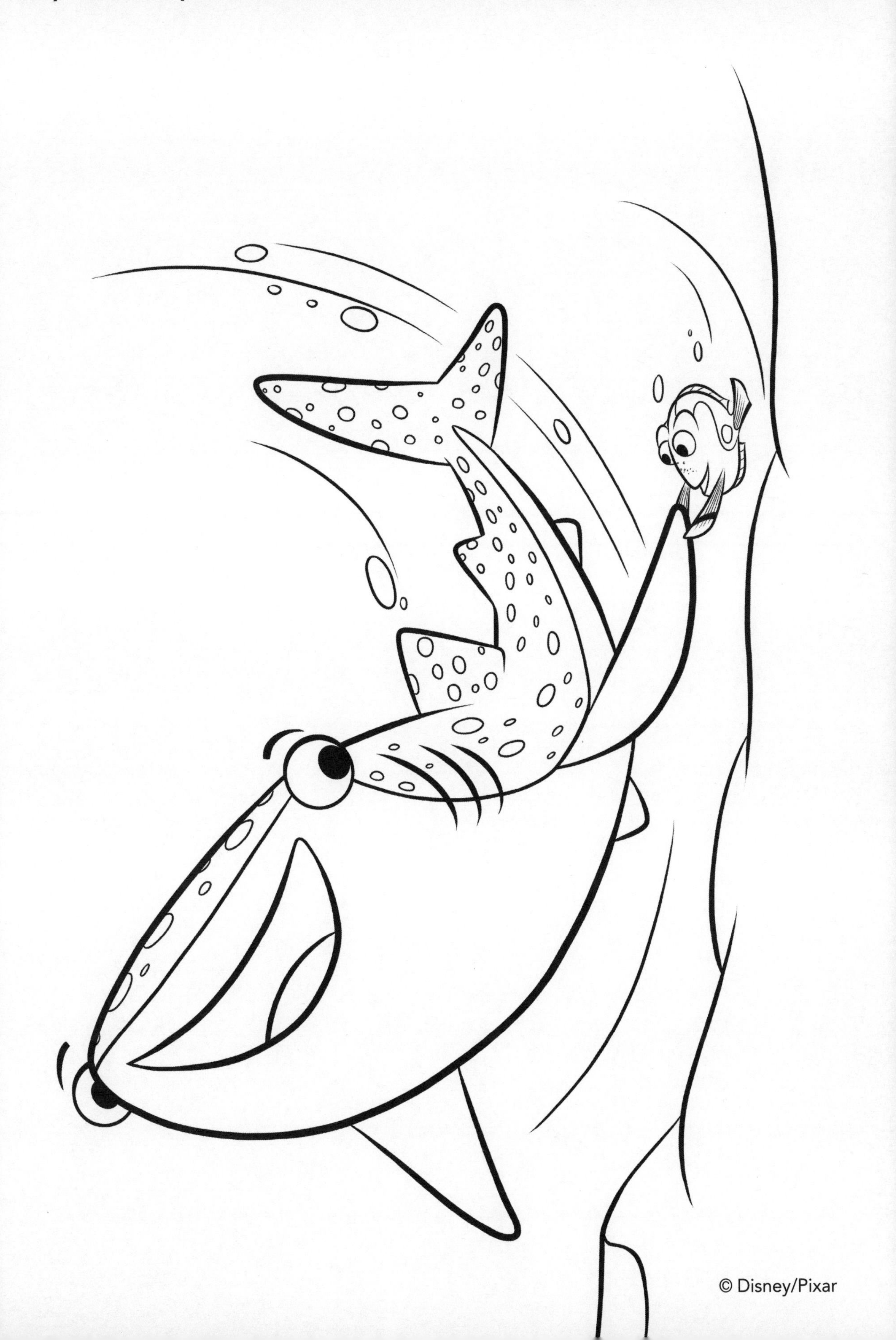

Bailey, a beluga whale, lives next door to Destiny. He's sick, so he can't use his echolocation skills to locate things far away.

Bailey and Destiny know where Dory's parents live! They tell Dory to go to an area called Open Ocean.

Meanwhile, Marlin and Nemo meet two sea lions named Fluke and Rudder. The sea lions offer to help them rescue Dory from the MLI!

Fluke and Rudder ask their friend Gerald if they can borrow his bucket.

A loon named Becky takes the bucket, scoops up Marlin and Nemo, and flies them toward the MLI.

Back inside the MLI, Destiny makes a big splash to help Dory and Hank escape through the crowd.

While Destiny distracts the crowd, Hank and Dory jump into a stroller and make their way to Open Ocean. Dory gives directions while Hank pushes.

Oh, no! Becky has left Marlin and Nemo in a tree!
How are they going to find Dory now?

On their way to Open Ocean, Hank and Dory fall into the touch pool! Dory tries to hide as dozens of little hands poke and prod the water.

Suddenly, Dory remembers her parents teaching her a special song, and she knows just what to do! "Just keep swimming, swimming. . . ."

Hank and Dory are safe. In the distance, Dory spots a sign for Open Ocean. "Home," she sighs with relief.

Finally, Marlin and Dory fall out of the tree and into a pool filled with robot fish . . . that look just like Dory!

Hank swings above Open Ocean, ready to throw Dory in.
Dory is excited—she's almost home!

Marlin and Nemo are still stuck in the robot fish tank, until Nemo asks, "What would Dory do?"

The two fish leap out of the tank and fly through the air! They land on a jet of water and bounce from stream to stream, making their way to the tidal pool.

In the tidal pool, Marlin and Dory meet a loudmouth clam. He loves to talk—a lot! How will they get away? "What would Dory do?" Marlin asks Nemo.

It's time for Dory to go home! Dory gives her tag to Hank so he can go to Cleveland. Hank says a sad goodbye, and then gently drops Dory in the tank.

3181

Dory gazes around Open Ocean—she made it!

Dory finds a trail of shells. She follows them one by one until she sees . . .

. . . her home! Dory calls out for her parents, but she can't find them. Another fish tells her that they've been taken to Quarantine— to be shipped to Cleveland!

Dory suddenly remembers that she got pulled away in the undertow when she was little. That's how she got lost!

Dory decides to go into the pipes to try and find her parents. But she quickly forgets her way and gets lost! Dory is about to give up hope when she remembers . . .

. . . Destiny! Together, Destiny and Bailey help Dory find her way through the pipes. Bailey's echolocation does work after all!

Suddenly, Dory bumps into two familiar fish . . . Marlin and Nemo! They swim through the pipes to Quarantine, where they find Hank.

With Hank's help, Dory looks into a tank of blue tangs, hoping to find her parents . . . but they're not there.

Oh, no! Hank gets startled and drops Dory! She flies through the air and falls down a drain that leads to the ocean.

In the ocean, Dory notices lots of paths made of shells, just like the ones near her home! She picks a path to follow. . . .

The path leads to Dory's parents! They've been waiting for her all this time, hoping she would find them.

Now that she's found her parents, Dory needs to rescue Marlin and Nemo before they're shipped to Cleveland! Bailey uses his echolocation to find them.

Dory and Hank find Marlin and Nemo
in a truck headed to Cleveland.

Becky the loon arrives to help carry
the fish to safety, but Dory gets left behind!

Hank distracts the truck drivers and then,
while they're not looking, jumps into the driver's seat!
He steers and pushes the pedals while Dory directs him.

Dory and Hank follow the seagulls and drive the truck all the way into the ocean. They're free!

Back in the ocean, Dory is reunited with Marlin, Nemo, and her parents. They all laugh and play together as one big, happy family.

Hank, Destiny, and Bailey decide to stay with Dory in the ocean. Hank becomes Nemo's new teacher, with Bailey and Destiny as his assistants!